The AMAZING DAYS of ABBY HAYES

Out of Sight, Out of Mind

Read more books about me!

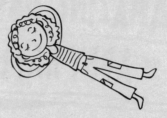

The AMAZING DAYS of ABBY HAYES

Out of Sight, Out of Mind

ANNE MAZER

AN
APPLE
PAPERBACK

SCHOLASTIC INC.
New York Toronto London Auckland Sydney
Mexico City New Delhi Hong Kong Buenos Aires

ISBN 0-439-35368-8

12 11 10 9 8 7 6   3 4 5 6 7/0

Printed in the U.S.A.

First printing, December 2002